HICCUP

by MERCER MAYER

The Dial Press 🦁 New York

Copyright © 1976 by Mercer Mayer · All rights reserved
First Printing · Printed in the United States of America
Library of Congress Cataloging in Publication Data
Mayer, Mercer, 1943— Hiccup.
Summary: Mr. Hippopotamus' violent efforts to
cure his lady friend's hiccups become increasingly
irritating to her—then he gets an attack.
[1. Stories without words. 2. Hiccups—Fiction.
3. Hippopotamus—Fiction] I. Title.
PZ7.M462Hi [E] 76-2284
ISBN 0-8037-3591-X ISBN 0-8037-3592-8 lib. bdg.

For Beverly and Gerald,
two dear friends